Little One Inch

Retold by Akimi Gibson

Illustrated by Megumi Akiyama

SCHOLASTIC INC.

New York Toronto London Auckland Sydney

Copyright © 1994 by Scholastic Inc.
All rights reserved. Published by Scholastic Inc.
Printed in the U.S.A.
ISBN 0-590-27570-4

2 3 4 5 6 7 8 9 10   09   00 99 98 97 96 95 94

Once upon a time in old Japan, there lived a kind man and woman. Their life was very peaceful. But they never had any children and this made them feel sad.

During the day, they worked their field.
During the night, they made their wish:

"Star light, star bright.
Please grant our wish tonight.
We wish for a sweet little child."

One morning when they were taking a walk, they heard a tiny little cry. They looked around to see where it was coming from. Hiding in the grass was a tiny little boy.

The man and woman were filled with joy
because their wish had come true.

They brought the tiny boy home and took care of him. As the years went by the boy was happy, but he never grew any bigger than an inchworm.

The boy became known as Little One Inch.
He was different, but he was loved by everyone.

One day when Little One Inch was in town, he heard a very loud sound. He looked around to see where it was coming from.

Then he saw the creature.

It was the biggest creature he had ever seen.
When the townspeople saw it, they ran away.
Everyone ran except Little One Inch.

Little One Inch knew he had to save the town. He quickly borrowed a spool of thread from the tailor and ran back to find the creature.

Because Little One Inch was so small, he was able to sneak up on the creature. He took his thread and ran around and around the creature's legs until the creature was all tied up.

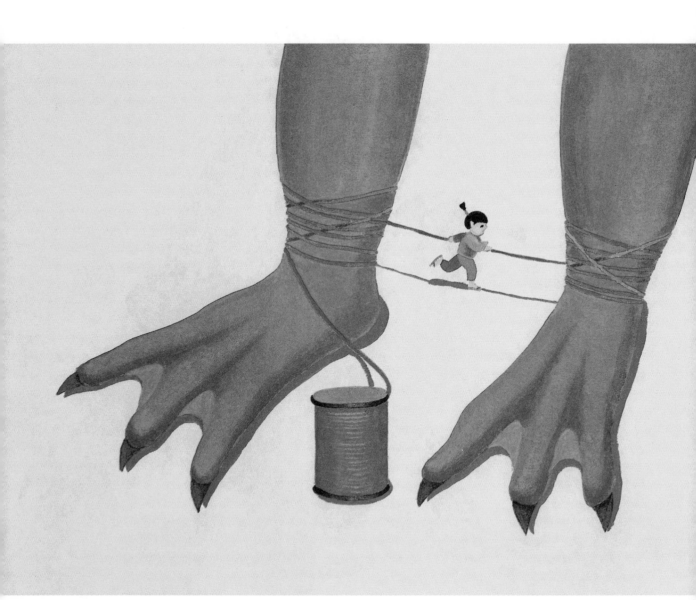

Then with all his might, he pulled the thread.
The creature fell to the ground with a loud
crash. When the creature looked up, it saw
Little One Inch.

"Why did you tie my legs?" the creature asked.

"I had to save the town from *you*," replied Little One Inch.

The creature became very sad. "I am a peaceful creature," it said. "I would not harm anyone."

Little One Inch thought about what the creature said. The creature was different, but so was Little One Inch. Then Little One Inch untied the creature.

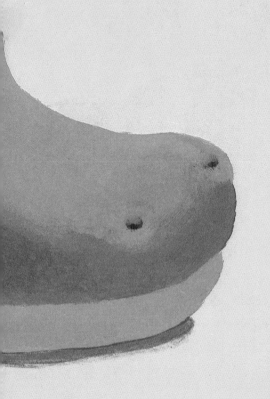

From that day on, one tiny little boy,
one very big creature, the kind man and woman,
and all the townspeople lived happily ever after.